THE
FRAY

Renn White

ONE

Blood curdling screams echoed through the woods, branches snapped under foot as the thin shadowy figure ran as fast as they could, their breath leaving clouds of condensation behind them in the chilly air.

When they finally stopped running the air was still and quiet around them. No light came from inside the trees, no more faint noises were heard.

But not for long. Suddenly something crashed through the foliage only a few yards behind, the beast scrambling over fallen logs, its teeth snapping at any obstacles it encountered on its way. When it had finally come to a stop, it looked around with a blood-curdling snarl, breathing heavily and panting. It shook off a layer of mud that had settled on it after covering several miles of forest ground.

It charged forwards on all fours like some fell beast out of a horror movie, a pair of glowing yellow eyes fixed on the figure before it. At the last minute before it struck, the figure spun around quickly, both arms swinging into action, one slamming into the creature's chest, the other smashing against its skull.

The sounds were incredible, reverberating throughout the area as if someone had struck a gong with steel hammers. The beast cried out in pain and rage and attacked again, but this time its movements seemed less precise, a lumbering staccato, broken bones grinding together within its deformed body.

At once, the figure began throwing defensive punches, feeling a satisfying connection each time one struck, connecting harder and faster as the creature grew weaker and wearier.

The figure grabbed its head by the fur, twisting the neck violently and thrusting their knee into its midsection. With one final swing they slammed the creature's face into a tree trunk, hearing bone snap under the force. They didn't even pause to take stock of the damage done; instead, swinging again they smashed the thing's head back into the tree, watching as a glint of metal burst through the skin and a fountain of blood sprayed up into the evening air.

"You're losing control," a voice called over the headset, and the person controlling the figure jumped in genuine shock, watching as an intruder materialized out of nowhere.

"Get a hold of yourself!"

Shaking their head, the figure forced themselves to focus, continuing to beat on the creature until the thing fell completely limp.

Moving to the creature's side, they flicked their arm, revealing a slender blade attached to their wrist by a flexible leather cord. Without a word the figure withdrew the weapon and sliced into the creature's throat, then plunged the blade into the thing's stomach and cut diagonally upwards into its rib cage.

Both made for heavy wet sounds as the creature struggled for a second before dying with a choked whimper. Blood and intestines fell to the earth with a sickening wet drop.

Grinning, Mike removed his helmet and turned around, finding two figures standing in the darkness behind him. He lowered his visor, slipping the clip that held his goggles down to his collar and let out a deep and contented sigh.

"Good game?" the overweight Rob asked as he took the VR headset from the dark-haired game tester, genuine concern on his features. "Honestly?"

"Man, that was pretty intense, it almost felt real," said Mike.

"Yeah," Tom agreed. "But how'd you know what to do?"

He shrugged. "I just guessed and kept playing."

Rob chuckled, his grin spreading across his face as he glanced at Tom. "Do you fancy a go on it?"

As Tom accepted the VR set with a grin, a wave of nausea hit Mike, causing him to grip his knees to prevent himself from dropping straight to the ground.

The video game simulation must have been a little more intense than he was used to.

"Mike? You okay man?" Rob moved to his side.

Mike blinked hard to clear his vision and glanced up at Rob, finding the game designer peering closely at him. The concern on Rob's face worried him, and he forced a smile to hide the fact that his heart was pounding rapidly in his chest. It didn't matter how good he got with video games, there was nothing he could do about his body being ill prepared for such intense situations in VR. In retrospect it probably wasn't wise to pick games that put so much stress on his system. Perhaps he should just stick to watching TV, although would that be entertaining enough?

In moments, he was fine, the nausea passing away, and he sat quietly while his friends chatted with each other, listening intently, occasionally offering helpful suggestions.

"The games almost set for release, just a couple of bugs to fix and we are good to go," Rob grinned, his face showing the excitement he felt, his eyes bright behind his round glasses.

"What kind of people are you hoping will want to play this game?" Mike's question drew the designer's attention.

"Everybody. "Rob shrugged. "Most MMORPGs are stuffed full of the same boring shit and full of pussies. This will be different. Trust me."

"Yeah?" Mike raised an eyebrow.

"Yeah, that's why the company is pushing out all these new games, we're trying to break the mould and bring something fresh to the table. We want people to make different choices than what they've always made."

"Could you make it even gorier?" Mike asked, genuinely curious. "Go more extreme than anyone else has before?"

Rob cocked his head to the side, thinking carefully. The idea sounded interesting, especially considering that the company he had designed the game for made their living off selling hardcore content to fans of blood and gore.

This game was different.

This was going to change lives.

He could feel it in his bones.

***

TWO

Three months passed and launch day finally arrived.

In the comfort of their own homes, the first of the players readied their machines, logged on to the network and within minutes people were running around in a new world, one that was meant to rival the real world.

Except something went wrong.

Within minutes players felt a sudden burn behind their eyes, their ears filled with the sounds of growls and snarls coming from nowhere. Blood started oozing from their ears, eyes, and noses as the sounds intensified. For hours they remained paralyzed, the audio continuing to flood their senses, bringing severe pain to anyone unlucky enough to be affected by it until finally, without any warning at all, everything went quiet.

Rising from the floor, dazed, and confused, Leia removed the headset, her eyes, nose, and ears covered in crusty dried blood and a metallic taste still lingering in her mouth. She tried to remember what had resulted in her waking up on the floor covered in blood, but her head felt full of cotton wool and the noises in the room around her sounded muffled as if she was listening from underwater. The room was much darker than when she had first slipped the headset on and launched the FRAY. Everything felt wrong and alien to her senses.

'What happened? Where am I?'

She blinked, then stared at her surroundings, taking in every detail of the room that was her current environment.

Everything looked the same just darker.

And yet she felt nothing, no connection between herself and the world around her.

As if nothing was real.

Had she gone crazy?

Had something gone wrong with the game?

Her headache persisted and with it came a constant sense of dread.

Leia fought the urge to bolt from the room, walking stiffly forward towards the door, but was halted by a sense of familiarity that seemed foreign at best. She started to remember little snippets of what had happened, she had just launched the game, created a character and was being hunted in the woods by something, suddenly a loud snarling sound and then she woke up on the floor, had that noise caused some sort of reaction, had she tried to flee whatever had made it and accidently fallen over in her room and knocked herself unconscious?

That had to be it. Surely.

Her stomach lurched as the contents rose, a combination of food and bile, filling her mouth.

Finally, unable to take the nausea anymore,

Leia staggered towards the bathroom, stopping to listen for noises before entering the room, wincing as the wooden floor creaked beneath her feet. Inside she splashed water on her face, giving it a cursory rinse, and put a hand on her forehead. She could feel her heartbeat throbbing painfully in her temple, blood pounding relentlessly in her ears. Leia opened her mouth, her stomach contents rushed up her throat, before ejecting with such force that they soaked the rim of the toilet bowl. The taste of bile left her feeling queasy as she threw up again, hands trembling with the effort of keeping her balance.

Finally, she collapsed into a heap on the wooden floor, still gasping and fighting for breath, letting out ragged wheezes.

For a minute or two she laid there, fighting the dull waves of dizziness that plagued her. She felt an overwhelming need to find food and drink, as if her entire being had been starved and now desperately craved sustenance, the hunger pains coursing through her body, attacking her insides with every breath she took. There was also a growing tension inside of her, almost unbearable, a strange inner sense that something was missing and wanted her attention urgently. After a few moments she decided she needed to push through the pain and find food.

Pushing herself to her feet she exited the bathroom and went back through to the kitchen. Her hands shook as she tore open a take-away carton of left over noodles from the previous night, the contents practically spilling out onto the counter. Leia devoured them without hesitation, her appetite soaring despite the raw feeling in her gut.

Her empty stomach finally relented and accepted the nourishment gratefully.

When her hands were no longer shaking Leia realized she was starving, despite the leftovers that she had just hungrily consumed. Her lips pressed together tightly, trying to quell a yawn that was threatening to come out. Feeling very tired, she turned around and slumped onto the chair, exhausted. She looked around for her phone, finally spotting it on the small dining table, next to a tall bottle of coke.

Dropping the remainder of the carton of noodles down onto the seat next to her, Leia sighed heavily, leaning back into the chair. Grabbing her phone up off the table she entered her pin and then hit the contacts before hesitating for a moment, considering what she was about to do. If anyone could help her figure out what had happened to her tonight, it would be Mike.

****

Three

The vibration of a phone sounded from the bedside table in a dimly lit room, the shape on the bed stirred slightly in their sleep before grunting awake. A pale hand reached across to snatch up the vibrating device, answering groggily.

"Hello."

"Hey dude, something weird happened when I launched FRAY, can we talk?" the familiar voice of Leia asked as her stomach lurched again as if calling to be fed.

"What do you mean?" Mike replied, half asleep.

"My head feels like someone dropped an anvil on it and my brain feels...off. I came to on the floor, blood all over my face and hours had passed."

"You must have taken a tumble."

"Not exactly." Leia replied, fighting back another wave of nausea.

"Then what do you mean?"

"I feel like I'm somewhere I don't know yet it's my own home." Leia paused, pulling the headset closer to her ear. "I feel like I've gone insane or something. Can you please help me find out what happened? I've never had this reaction to a game."

Mike hesitated before answering, now awake and sitting propped up in bed, a concerned look upon his face. He hadn't expected to hear from her after all these weeks, he didn't know what she knew about the beta test or his reaction to the game. After their relationship had ended, he never thought he would hear from her again. Yet here she was, calling him in the middle of the night, asking for his help.

"How much do you remember?" he asked.

"Just bits and pieces really, I remember a sudden sharp pain in my eyes and then a growling and snarling, like something was coming for me. Then I woke up on the floor." Leia explained.

"Did you try to fight off whatever it was?"

"No! I never had time. Before I even had a chance to react the sound intensified until it felt like someone dropped an anvil on my head, it must have knocked me out cold," Leia paused, contemplating her words, trying to ignore the nausea in her gut.

Mike responded slowly, not surprised at all, in fact fully expecting her response. "What happened to you after you woke?"

"I got nauseous, and I stumbled into the bathroom, ended up throwing up, barely got enough food down before I threw up again. Now I feel like death warmed up. Do you have any idea what caused it?"

"I do. You tripped and fell. Nothing unusual about that. Some players suffer those nasty sensations when they trip over something on the level. Some gamers spend years complaining about them."

"Really?! So, it's just normal for that to happen?" Leia replied sceptically, and he could picture her shaking her head at his explanation.

"Yeah, completely normal. You probably just got attacked by one of the creatures from behind and your brain filled in the blanks but most likely there was a simulation error," he chuckled.

"So, nothing unusual happened. I just got hurt because of a simulation error."

"Well simulations aren't perfect. Things do fail. We fixed all the bugs but obviously we can't control user error. We do include warnings to say be aware of your surroundings to try and warn people."

"Don't patronise me Mike," Leia growled as she felt a rush of anger wash over her, followed by a vision of her grabbing him by the throat and biting his lip hard between her teeth, clamping down until the skin started to give way beneath her grip. She shuddered at the image of the salty, metallic red fluid coursing through his veins rushing to the surface pooling in her mouth as she tore a chunk of pink, ragged flesh from his mouth. Savouring the taste and texture. Her vision darkened slightly at the image, and nausea washed over her once again.

"I'm done talking to you," she said as she hit the end call button, rushing across the dimly lit kitchen to the sink full of dirty dishes to throw up the noodles that she had consumed minutes before.

Gagging at the sour taste in her mouth, she tried to process the rage and thoughts that had just gone through her mind, the way it made her feel, the thought of biting and ripping off that tender pink flesh. Her stomach let out a growl, hunger coursed through her once again but this time it was different.

This time it was more of a need.

An urgent and powerful desire to consume something, to fill her stomach and keep it there, a cold feeling coursing through her, a sense of power tingling in her head. Leia shivered and began to vomit again.

She couldn't hold anything back now, even when nothing remained in her stomach it churned upwards, bile spilling over her lips.

Leia bent over and pressed the back of her hand against her chest, trying to slow the pulsing beat inside her body, trying to stop the tide of hunger surging through her system. But her efforts were futile, the sensation only increasing in intensity and strength until eventually they became overwhelming.

With a grunt she fell to her knees, blinking in confusion as a voice seemed to whisper in the recess of her mind, telling her to get back online to play FRAY once more, promising her that the hunger she felt was nothing more than a side effect of the need to immerse herself in the virtual world once more.

FOUR

Over the course of the next week, millions of players logged on to the FRAY, diving eagerly into the world with their avatars. There were widespread complaints from workplaces and schools about a severe lack of attendance, and the papers picked up the story and ran with it for a few days, but no-one really cared.

They were busy exploring the world of FRAY.

So desperate was their need to play the game; many of them becoming too engrossed that they hardly slept or used the bathroom, some merely placing a bucket next to where they were gaming.

As if the headsets had become part of them.

The new world of the FRAY had become the most important thing in their lives, and on the rare occasions that they left it they found themselves filled with an unspeakable rage and hate.

The world was addictive, leaving the players feeling more alive than they had in their real lives, filling them with a hunger for adventure and a blood lust for violence that they had never known before.

Leia had lost a week to the FRAY, her complexion had paled considerably in the time since the terrifying incident on launch day and her body was starting to show signs of exhaustion but no matter what she couldn't switch off.
She *needed* to level up her avatar.
It felt like it was the only thing that was keeping her crippling headache and nausea at bay.
A sudden pounding upon her front door snapped her back from the game into the real world. Removing the headset and placing it on the table beside her, Leia stumbled groggily toward the door, bouncing off the sofa as she went, her frail figure almost falling before regaining her balance.
"I'm fucking coming for god's sake, you can have the door when it comes off," Leia yelled as she staggered down the corridor, the thin wooden door shaking in its frame as the pounding continued. She yanked it open to find Mike standing there with a concerned look on his face, a hand raised to knock.
"Where the fuck have you been, I've been calling and texting you all week!"
"I've been playing FRAY, what's up?" Leia

snapped in confusion, wondering why on Earth her whereabouts mattered to her ex in the slightest.

She glanced over at the headset laying upon the table, trying to ignore the growing ache in her skull that was driving her insane with each passing second as she realised, she *should* be playing on it.

Mike stared at her in a mixture of shock and horror as he took in her complexion and shoddy appearance. Leia had always taken immense pride in how she looked, but today standing in her doorway she looked dishevelled in her dirty stained clothes, her skin pale and almost transparent and her face thin and gaunt with sunken in eyes.

"Jesus Leia, when was the last time that you showered?" Mike grimaced as the stench of sweaty fried onions emanated from Leia's armpits.

She ignored him as she began to pace around the room, a hand clasped to her head as she tried to get the throbbing in her forehead to calm down.

"Come on, what do you want? I need to get back to the game," Leia said edging closer to the table and the headset once more, desperate to continue playing, even though she knew that by doing so she was ignoring everything else in her life.

Everything apart from FRAY.

FRAY was all she had, all she needed.

"I looked into what you said about the noise and blacking out on launch day, something didn't seem right with what you said, so I checked the reports from that day," Mike replied, his voice sounding calmer than Leia had ever heard before.

"I went through them with the techs and at first glance they showed no indications of a glitch or error that would lead to that sort of behaviour, however when I delved a little deeper, I noticed a few odd lines of code, it seems that someone had logged on and created a back door to allow a virus into the system. The incident that happened was the result of a glitch caused by that backdoor being created."

She stopped pacing and turned to look at him with wide eyes, seeing the pity and disgust etched on his features as he stood studying her appearance.

"Is that bad?" she whispered, curious to hear the answer. "I mean, honestly, is it?"

Mike sighed wearily. "It seems the virus made the game more addictive and then it vanished."

"Why would someone create a virus like that?"

"There are millions of accounts within the game that haven't logged off since launch day and we think the person responsible might still be around somewhere in the system. I want you to keep away from the console at least for a couple of days," Mike replied solemnly, moving his hands in front of himself to calm Leia down, lowering his voice to a whisper as if he were in fear of being overheard.

"That sounds like you don't want me to play FRAY anymore," Leia stated, anger starting to rise within her as she stared back at Mike accusingly.

"That is not what I'm saying," Mike snapped in reply, shaking his head as though Leia had challenged him on his word. He paused for a moment before continuing, looking down at the floor.

"Look at the state of yourself Leia, you look like you haven't eaten in days, you certainly haven't washed in a few days, and you haven't stopped glancing at the headset on the table since I arrived. You need to stop playing."

"What?" she shook her head. "Fuck you."

Mike nodded as if expecting that reply, his eyes drifting to settle on the headset, then he started towards it, a hand reaching. "I'll take this then."

Leia rushed at the table, throwing herself at the headset before Mike could reach it, her hands clasping it to her body like a mother with a baby.

"Fuck you! If you come near me ever again I will fucking kill you!" Leia seethed venomously.

"Listen to yourself?" Mike shook his head at her. "You'll kill me…you need to stop playing now!"

With a snarl, she surged forward, swinging her hand out toward Mike's face, the headset smashing him hard in the right cheek, the plastic cracking in two pieces before Leia realised what she had done.

Now she could no longer enter FRAY.

Gasping in pain, Mike bent over, one hand clasping his cheek only to glance up as she rushed him. Leia raised her fist high above her head and began slamming her knuckles against Mike's face, desperately trying to break the bones within his cheeks and crush his nose in to pulp. Cursing, Mike backed away, tripping on his own feet and falling heavily to the carpet. Instantly Leia jumped upon him, grasping clumps of his thick brown hair between her fingers as she screamed at him and repeatedly slammed her head into his forehead before letting go and moving swiftly across the floor, snatching the mobile phone that lay upon the sofa and hurling it at him. Mike flinched away in time, the phone crashing into the wall behind him.

"Leia, for fuck's sake, stop this!" Mike pleaded frantically as she charged back towards him with murderous rage in her eyes. Her blonde hair whipping about in the air as she thrashed her head, her teeth gnashing together furiously, she lashed out at him with both her fists, every strike seeming to hammer a nail further into the coffin of his sanity.

"I need to play the Fray!" Leia yelled, her tears

welling in her eyes as she swung her arm out and shoved the thumbs of her hands into Mike's eyes.

He cried out, batting her hands aside and she snarled like an animal as she wrapped her fingers about his throat, squeezing as hard as she could.

Through the red haze of her rage, she saw the pain written upon Mike's face as if she were watching in third person, and she knew then that she had hurt him, but she had no control over her actions.

All she could think about was how he had stopped her playing her game, taken her away from FRAY and she wanted to hurt him, kill him even.

Struggling to free her hands from his throat, Mike's mind raced to find a way to calm her down and bring her back to her senses.

This was so unlike her.

In all the years he had known her she had never showed any form of violence and wouldn't even kill a fly or spider and he always joked about how she would catch them and set them free.

But now Mike could see the violence lying deep within her soul and its fury terrified him.

Without warning, the storm broke, the anger washing from Leia as if someone had pulled a plug from a bathtub and Leia staggered back from Mike and slumped back against the wall, shuddering as another bout of nausea rolled through her body.

Barely conscious, as weak as a kitten, she didn't resist as Mike crouched before her and gently lifted her up in his arms. Grim-faced, Mike carried her to the sofa and laid her upon it before dragging a throw rug across her legs, wrapping her tightly in it before sitting next to her, concern on his features.

Leia tried to speak but the words wouldn't come, her body trembling uncontrollably, her breaths shortening as the guilt grew deeper inside her.

She had hurt Mike, had wanted to kill him.

As Mike sat patiently by Leia's side, he watched as she struggled to keep her breathing steady, her fingers moving to her temples as if she were suffering a severe headache. Their eyes met and she winced.

"I'm sorry. I don't know what came over me, I have never felt so much rage before, it was as if I had no control over my own body."

Mike nodded, watching as she yawned and closed her eyes, her body relaxing as sleep took her.

He sat with her for several hours before Leia stirred, beginning to rouse herself from her coma-like state. When she did so, Mike gently helped her to sit up, watching her with concern.

He rested a comforting hand upon hers, squeezing it tenderly and smiling as he watched her struggle to regain some composure. Leia glanced at Mike with a sad smile, her head shaking in remorse.

"Thank you for staying," she spoke softly.

Mike nodded and glanced up to the wall clock, seeing that it was past midnight then he cleared his throat. "So… what should we do now?"

"I can't play the game, anymore," Leia stated, her finger trailing along the arm of the sofa as she contemplated her options, the thought of not being able to do so making her feel nauseous again. "I think it made me do those things to you, I can't explain it exactly but it kind of felt like somehow I was being controlled, like I was my own character, the anger I felt when I realised, I could no longer log back on was uncontrollable and all I could think was to kill you for taking the game away."

As she fell silent, her gaze far drifted to settle upon the broken headset now lying upon the floor.

"What are you saying…" Mike frowned.

Leia stood up and began to walk towards the broken headset, she picked it up from the floor and tossed it onto the sofa. "I think the incident on launch day had something to do with what just happened, as that night when I rang you something similar happened, when I was talking to you on the phone I started to become angry, I started to imagine myself biting you, ripping your lip off, my inner voice pleaded with me to play the game again and I did, and the anger went away."

Mike swallowed at her words, watching Leia as she sat down on the sofa and buried her head in her hands. For a moment, he thought she was crying but then she gazed up at Mike and spoke quietly, her voice breaking as she attempted to contain her emotions.

"I know it doesn't make sense, but I can't help thinking that somehow the game changed me somehow, made me lose control and attack you without warning. I can feel it whenever I think about the world, it's like there is something pulling at me from within."

Mike remained silent as he listened to her. Her story seemed so unreal that he doubted what she was telling him, yet he had seen her rage.

A notification coming through on his phone broke the silence, the chirping noise drawing both their attentions. Reaching into his pocket, Mike grasped his phone and pulled it out, swiping to unlock the screen and opening the notification, his brow furrowing as he read it.

It was a breaking news report, detailing an attack that had occurred earlier that day where a teenager had been arrested after a concerned neighbour had called to report a disturbance. Upon arrival at the scene, the police officers had discovered a fourteen-year-old crouching beside the body of their mother covered in blood. Upon further investigation, it was revealed that the teenager had beaten her to death with their games console after they had returned home to discover that he was not allowed to play the FRAY due to his behaviour.

Licking at his dry lips, Mike thumbed through the other news reports, seeing similar incidents of violence being reported from other teenage players. Mike sat back for a moment, processing what he had just read, the incident described in the articles had all been to do with FRAY. Was it possible that somehow the computer virus that made the game, so addictive had altered the minds of the players?

Maybe this was part of it, the game changing their processing and making them violent.

Rob had always joked the brain was just a fleshy computer waiting to be hacked and all it needed was for a bio engineered virus to come along, infect the damn thing and turn people mad. Maybe it was just that easy. Mike had an uneasy feeling running through him as he thought about the events of that night.

He needed to speak to Rob, and soon.

****

Five

Scratching at the pale hairy flesh of his gelatinous stomach that hung from the bottom of his grey food encrusted t shirt, Rob chuckled at the sitcom he was currently watching on tv. He had been holed up in his basement for a week now working on new game code and tinkering with the old one, the space heater set to max as he stared at the monitor displaying lines of digital code on an infinite white canvas. The company had tasked him with creating supplements to add to the game to draw even more players to FRAY, not happy with the millions who had already joined.

It was his favourite task as it gave him the opportunity to work alone and focus on what he enjoyed most, programming. His eyes twitched over to the email icon in the corner of his display which displayed numerous unread emails, but he chose to ignore them. He knew he should have been in the bunker with the rest of the team, but he preferred to work from home away from all the noise. Besides since release day he wanted to be as far away from the bunker, the programmers nickname for head office, as possible. The company wanted everyone to play the game, but he knew better. After all he was the one who had created it and he knew what was coming. He was going to take a back seat and let others run the show.

His mind snapped back to reality when he heard the front doorbell ringing, and he groaned aloud. He did not really want anyone interrupting him but had forgotten to turn the bell off. Snorting and pushing his keyboard back onto the table, he left his chair and walked upstairs. Passing the kitchen on the way to the front of the house, Rob grabbed a beer from the fridge before finally answering the door.

"Hey, sorry I didn't hear the bell." he said in a light friendly manner, glancing around the door to find a bruised Mike standing there, a pale almost anorexic looking blonde standing beside the programmer.

"We need to talk," Mike said sharply, a nod of his head gesturing to the woman. "This is Leia."

"The Leia?" Rob grinned. "The ex?"

Mike sighed. "We really need to talk with you."

Rob raised an eyebrow in curiosity but remained silent and ushered them both into the lounge, shutting the door behind them all. Joining them, he turned on the TV and selected a comedy as he opened the beer.

"Have a seat," he said waving at a large leather sofa. Mike and Leia made their way over and sat themselves down, while Rob took a seat opposite them, sipping at his beer. "It's a bit early to be calling a meeting."

"You are aware of what happened launch day aren't you?" Mike started, shaking his head in disbelief.

"Yes," Rob answered quietly, unsure why they were here asking him about it. "What's the problem?"

"We can't just ignore this!" Mike shook his head angrily. "You can't try and brush that shit under the carpet! People died because of what you did!"

Rob shrugged and put his beer down. "What do you want me to say? I am sorry. I didn't do anything other than fix a couple of bugs in a game and release it for the company. I did what I was paid to do."

He paused for a moment before continuing, studying the faces of his unexpected guests. "Yeah, there were deaths, but it was unintentional and unavoidable. It happens with all games. Some guy had an aneurysm while testing Mortal Kombat back in the day!"

"That's a bullshit urban legend," Mike shook his head.

Rob shrugged. "Whatever, bottom line is these things happen. Its expected. Collateral damage and all that."

Leia looked across at Mike, who frowned at his words, seemingly uncomfortable with the conversation as Robb continued. "The head of the company told us, all of us when we were hired, you knew the possible side effects of the game during development."

Leia could not believe what she was hearing.

Mike had known that this game would cause people to become so addicted they would become violent.

Seeing the worry on Leia's face, Mike tried to calm her. "Leia please let me explain, it's not what it sounds like, the company informed us that the game would be a very immersive experience and could have some side effects to the players health. Yes, people might die during gameplay and suffer cardiac arrest or similar, but that's only for underlying health conditions. The game had a warning, and it would be their choice whether to use the game or not."

Leia frowned. "So, you knew about the virus?"

"No, I didn't," he shook his head, turning to his colleague. "Rob you are the only one who would have been capable to write code this complex? Why did you agree to add this virus?"

"Well, the game has done pretty well. It has sold millions. So, what if people are spending too much time playing it. That's the reason I agreed to make it. I realised that the rush of dopamine released by the subliminal message in the coding would drive people mad with addiction. That's what the company wanted. Its what they paid me to do. They thought having it be so addictive would ensure people spent more time on FRAY than in the real world." Rob finished bitterly. "They made millions from this. It's the highest selling game in its first week of release!"

Leia interjected; her voice shaky. "This means the game controls people instead of them controlling it, so the rage comes from the game not from them?"

"Did you say the game is making people angry?" Rob asked, shaking his head. "It can't be. For it to be affecting people's emotions and causing extreme rage it would have to be altering the functioning of the amygdala, but that would make sense I guess as that also plays a part in addiction. I mean if enough dopamine was introduced then suddenly taken away it could make a person to crave more, but the effects would soon wear off. We all know that addiction causes the patient to start acting irrationally."

Leia and Mike shared confused looks, as Rob continued. "There wouldn't be a lasting effect from the anger building up over the last few days, it would burn itself out eventually. However, if somehow the virus managed to make the jump from machine to human, then maybe, just maybe it's possible that it would have long lasting effects."

"He's saying this game is like crack for our brains, isn't he?" Leia whispered in disgust as she glanced at Mike.

"I'm glad you guys are sitting down," Rob began, ignoring her reaction. "Now listen carefully to what I'm gonna tell you OK. This game was designed to keep players wanting more, to be almost unable to function in the real world and spend almost every minute of their time in FRAY."

Mike felt like his head was spinning, unable to process the information given to him. Could it really be true? He looked across at Leia who stared ahead as if lost in her own thoughts, her lips clamped together.

Rob continued. "The longer the duration of playing FRAY, the more difficult it will be to stop playing and now that FRAY has been made available online for free, people will probably find themselves constantly craving to play more."

"What are you saying?" Leia asked, letting her gaze settle back on him, a concerned look in her eyes.

"The longer the player is exposed to FRAY, the worse it gets, it keeps pushing for more until finally the addiction becomes impossible to break, you simply can't leave FRAY," Rob answered gravely. "As such you will keep turning to the game to cope with stress, to relieve pain or just simply because your brain needs the stimulus."

Leia stood up abruptly and paced around the room muttering to herself. "If this is true it needs to be stopped before it gets any worse. The news is reporting kids are killing people over this game!"

Mike stood up and took a deep breath. "Leia's right, we need to warn people! There is no way they're gonna get away with this, they can't control people!"

"Listen," Rob interrupted. "This game is about experiences, it's not about controlling people, how many times have you heard someone say they wanted to try something for the first time in their life? You might feel weird at first but it's only natural, in fact I'd bet money that the vast majority of people wish they were able to live life the way FRAY allows."

Leia ignored him. "Please mike we need to put a stop to this before it gets any worse, I have experienced the rage this game causes, the lack of control…I tried to kill you for fuck's sake. Imagine what would happen if we let this continue."

"If we took the servers offline it would kick everybody out of the system," Mike exclaimed. "There is no way in hell we're letting this continue. We have to pull the plug before it gets any worse."

Rob let out a chuckle. "You are still looking at this all wrong, it has never been about controlling people, the virus can't infect people, it's just subliminal messages telling people to play and only think about playing FRAY nothing more."

Leia gasped. "You are an arsehole. How could you do this to millions of people and not have any remorse?"

"I'm not doing anything. I'm just the programmer," he said shrugging his shoulders, clearly unrepentant.

Mike sighed, watching as Leia and Rob stood staring each other down, his mind in overdrive trying to think of how to even process what to do next.

"Tell me something, are you too stupid to realise the danger you're putting others in? Or are you seriously so blind you don't see with what you're doing?" she demanded spitting venom as she glared back at Rob.

He shrugged, unconcerned.
He had known what he was doing and the risks that came with it, but the company had paid him an

exceptionally large bonus. Money was all he needed in his life.

SIX

Mike knew that the only way to stop the outbursts of violence was to take the server down, but to do that he needed to get to the bunker and pull the plug. And even then, there was no guarantee that it wouldn't spread further into the system, which meant that turning the server off might have no effect at all.

He needed to disable the network immediately, before it got any worse. Without a thought of what Rob may do in response, he headed for the door, Leia following.

Throwing open the door to his car, he climbed in and stared back at the house they had just left with disgust, the respect he had for his friend now completely gone.

Leia climbed into the passenger seat beside him, shut her door and turned on the radio, a soft female voice emerging from the speakers to break the silence.

"We are going to put a stop to this," Mike grunted as he started the engine and reversed out of the drive, Leia nodding at his words, but unsure how.

As he pulled onto the main road he glanced at the dashboard clock, saw that it had just gone midday, and cast a glance at Leia. "It's about a half hour drive to the bunker, then..."

His words trailed off as he suddenly turned up the radio, his brow furrowing as he listened to the DJ as she began to speak again. "...the number of violent attacks being reported are growing exponentially and are all reported to be linked to some new video game. Here at Talk radio, we want to know what you guys think. Call in on 0331 839 5780 and let us hear your thoughts on the topic."

"Shall I call in?" Leia asked, wondering if warning the public would be the best way to handle the situation.

"Probably best not to. They will think you are a flat earth conspiracy nut," he replied with a grim smile.

Leia ignored the smile and turned the radio up a bit louder so the engine noise could no longer be heard over it as the DJ spoke again. "And we have Vincent on line one, what's your thought on the attacks?"

"It's crazy!" the man named Vincent came on the line to the DJ. "The whole thing must be some kind of hoax! Nothing but lazy rude kids with no discipline that need a good beating just like we got as kids. That will sort them all out!"

"Come on now Vincent," the presenter's tone shifted slightly. "I don't doubt that we all had some bad moments in our childhood but nothing like what these kids are reported to be doing."

There was a pause and the voice of the DJ returned we've got another caller waiting on line two. Thank you for joining us today."

"A pleasure," what sounded like a teenager replied. "My name is Jasper."

"Tell me Jasper, how do you think this game has affected people, have they changed at all since its release?" the DJ asked, and the young man on the line sounded scared, his voice shaking as he answered.

"Uhm…I…!" he trailed off nervously. "It....has affected my flatmates, they have become very angry lately and they don't seem to care anymore about anything other than playing the game."

"Can you give me an example?" the DJ asked.

"Uhm, well, uhm they haven't been going out anymore, we used to go everywhere together but now it's just me, they won't come out of the flat, ever. I'm worried for them," Jasper explained, sounding like he wanted to add more to his statement but was not sure how to proceed. "I'm beginning to wonder if it's safe for me to be around them anymore. One of them threatened to rip my face off when I tried to tell them the game was stupid."

"That sounds pretty extreme," the DJ stated.

A gasp sounded across the airwaves, followed by Jasper's voice as he addressed someone. "Wait, what are you doing in here, wait please.... stop......."

There was a muffled scream followed by a wet thunk sound that filled the car from the radio, and then the DJ began to call the man's name repeatedly.

SEVEN

Mike pulled the steering wheel sharply left sending the car skidding in against the kerb. throwing Leia jerking forward towards the dashboard, stopped by her seatbelt. Reaching out with a hand, Mike switched off the radio and sat silent for a moment, while Leia sat with a hand covering her mouth, her eyes glued to the windscreen staring straight ahead at the passing cars on the road. "Jesus Christ, you nearly killed me!"

Mike took a deep breath and glanced sideways at her. "What the hell just happened? On the radio!"

She held his gaze, unspeaking as she considered what they had both heard, the screaming and the wet thunking noise replaying over and over in her mind.

Leia wondered if Mike knew more than he was telling her, brow furrowing as something occurred to her. "Why didn't you play the game on release day?"

"What?" Mike repeated bewildered by the change in subject. "How do you know I didn't."

"I phoned you remember; you seemed fine."

"Why does that matter now?"

"Tell me why?" she repeated more forcefully.

Mike stared at her for a moment and let out a sigh and cleared his throat. "Honestly, I played it enough during the testing stage to not need to play it again, the game was just like all the others, mediocre."

Leia glared at him furiously, she felt a cold rage inside that threatened to consume her as she considered his words, certain now that he *was* lying to her. They sat silently for a long moment as the anger built in her, then she found her voice again. "You are lying to me. You really expect me to believe you didn't know about this virus being planted in the game?"

"Do you really think if I had any input in this virus, I would be here now trying to stop it?" he snapped at her, but she was staring blankly out the window. "Rob admitted it was him. You heard him!"

She nodded at his words and fell silent again.

Starting the car again, Mike drove onwards, steering them through the streets of London until they finally reached their destination. Over fifteen mins had passed with neither saying a word to each other.

"We're here," Mike exclaimed as he pulled into an underground carpark, waiting as the barriers lifted to allow them entry. The thick concrete walls, poorly lit by fluorescent lighting, cast strange shadows on the pavement below making it feel almost creepy, the damp atmosphere added to the feeling. Mike parked in his usual spot and they both headed to the lobby entrance, neither knowing what to expect when they entered the building or what they were going to do.

"Good afternoon," a grim-faced security guard greeted them as he opened the door for the pair, a second guard seated behind the reception desk watching a tv monitor, drinking from a cup.

Mike smiled in reply, showed him an ID card, and they made their way through the lobby, passing several people in suits who looked like they were on their way back to their offices in the building above.

"When you said the bunker, I expected some sort of underground military style bunker not a huge office building in the middle of the city," Leia marvelled as she watched people hurry by with their Starbucks coffee cups and their takeout lunches. Mike smiled at her words, leading her onwards as they walked past the reception and down the hallway, until finally they arrived at the correct elevator, where a young man stood waiting beside the call button, his black hood pulled up over his head, music blaring from underneath it. The call button flashed for a moment and as the doors slid open with a soft chime, the young man in the hoodie entered, pressed a button and moved to stand at the back. Exchanging glances, Mike and Leia boarded the elevator, neither of them speaking as the music from the young man's hood continued to blare away. Shaking his head, Mike went to press the button for the sixth floor, saw that it was already illuminated and then stepped back beside Leia.

The elevator lurched several times as it made its way up through the building, and Leia grabbed hold of the handrail that ran around the interior as if she were expecting it to suddenly drop and fall at any moment.

At last, the elevator doors slid open, and Mike and Leia stepped out to look around at the dark corridors, a pair of fluorescent strip lights above cast a dim yellow glow in the gloom, which did little to illuminate the drab grey walls and carpet. The young man in the hoodie stepped past them, and hurried down the corridor, before throwing open a door to what Mike knew to be the staff room and then heading inside.

The office was deathly quiet, the buzz of human chatter that they had heard downstairs replaced by an eerie silence that caused Leia's heartbeat to quicken.

"This way," Mike started to head down the corridor, but Leia paused, peering in through a crack in the office door beside her, her brow furrowing as she tried to absorb the scene before her within it.

A lone man stood in front of a wall mounted TV playing FRAY, his blue jeans stained with varying shades of brown and green, the overwhelming stench of ammonia and faeces hung heavy in the air.

Leia felt a wave of nausea rise-up her throat at the smell, but deep within her mind she could feel the need to play FRAY growing again, the throbbing pain in her head starting to niggle away, rubbing at her temples she quickly stepped away from the door.

Hurrying down the corridor to catch up with Mike, she found him standing outside of another office, presumably the one that he had worked in, the same stench Leia had just been subjected to moments prior now saturating the air around them. As she clapped a hand to her mouth and nostrils, Mike turned to grimace at her. "What the fuck is that?"

She shook her head, gesturing back the way that they had come. "I have just seen someone along there in an office playing FRAY and I can only assume from the smell of them none stop for a very, very, long time. The guy was wearing shit and piss-stained trousers."

Casting her a stunned look, Mike opened the door before them, and they were greeted with a similar sight. A pallid faced Tim was stood in front of the monitor, the glow from the headset illuminating his sunken in cheeks and cracked lips, the smell was coming from a bucket beside the desk, which was overflowing on to the carpet, chunks of faeces floating atop it, the acrid stench of ammonia stinging at their eye and throats.

"Dude what the fuck!" Mike shouted. "Tim?"

Tim never said a word, and just carried on playing his game, seemingly oblivious to the fact that Mike and Leia were in the office, his eyes locked to the monitor.

"We need to shut this shit down, we can't waste any more time," Mike grunted as he moved to a desk and began searching through a drawer. "I need to find the key card for the server room. Rob used to keep it stashed in here with all his other shit."

Pulling a second drawer, he gave a grunt of triumph and snatched up the card. "Come on Leia!"

Together they made their way out of the room and began heading further down the corridor, passing numerous offices of people all sat playing FRAY, each of those gaming acting as if they were unaware anyone else was in the building with them, their attention locked onto the flashing monitors before them.

Yet these people did not have buckets like Tom had, and their trousers were thick with stains and filth.

Grim-faced the pair hurried on to the server room, where Mike fished in his pocket again for the key card.

"Hold on," he told Leia as he swiped the card into the slot triggering the magnetic locks and allowing the pair entrance to the room that sat waiting beyond them. Once inside the pair closed the door behind them and looked around to get their bearings, the entire room was lined with row upon row of servers of varying sizes all running FRAY, their electrical hum loud.

"Holy shit this is what a server farm looks like," Leia said stunned as she turned on the spot, examining the many lights blinking on the various terminals lining the walls. "How do we take them offline."

"Unplug as many as you can," Mike told her grimly. "We will need to start an electrical fire somehow to destroy them completely but for now this will get everyone offline and stop them playing the FRAY."

"A fire?" she shook her head. "Arson?"

Mike nodded. "Yeah, prison time if we get caught but what's the alternative? People will hopefully thank us."

Without waiting for her to reply, Mike strode over to a bank of machines labelled Alfa-One to Kilo-One and opened an electrical panel on the wall situated halfway down their length. Pointing with a finger, he told Leia to move to a similar electrical box further down between machines labelled Lima-One to Zulu-One.

Opening the box before him, Mike stared inside at the contents for a moment, brow furrowing then nodded over at Leia. "Rip out all of the green wires."

"Are you sure?" she was suddenly nervous.

"Trust me," he wished he sounded more confident as he reached inside and yanked cables loose, a curse of dread and pain escaping him each time they sparked.

EIGHT

At once the hum of the servers began to fade, the flashing lights upon each of the machines blinking off, to be replaced by an almost animal like scream.

"What the fuck was that?" Leia shot Mike a glance of concern, the pair stepping back towards the door just in time to see the young man they had been in the lift with running up to the door, a look of pure terror etched on his face, his hand jerking the handle.

"What's he doing?" Leia winced. "Does he know what we've done? Mike, what's going on?"

"I don't know," he shook his head, dragging the key card from his pocket and sliding it through the lock. As Mike swiped the card, the latch on the door finally released, swinging wide open and the young man cast a look over his shoulder at the corridor behind him then tumbled through the door, falling on to the floor.

"Hey dude," Mike frowned as he bent to help him to his feet, Leia helping him as the young man began to jerk and writhe in terror, desperate to get in the room.

All three of them cursed as they rose and found the grime-stained figure of Tom now standing in the open doorway, his features appearing sunken in like an addict, blood oozing from his eyes, nose, and ears as he stood there snarling at them like a rabid animal.

"Tom snap out of it" Mike cried out as Tom growled again, then suddenly lunged forward towards the young lad, dirty hands grasping for his clothing.

Somehow, Mike managed to drag the hoodie wearing youngster out of the way, sending Tom crashing past them to collide heavily with the now inactive servers.

With a snarl that sent drool and blood splattering across the floor of the server room, Tom surged back to his feet with an athleticism that Mike had never seen his friend display and charged at the youngster again, this time grabbing him by the hood, yanking him back. Stunned, Mike rushed forward, grabbing Tom by the waist, desperately dragging him off the screaming young man who now sported a wet patch on the front of his jeans, throwing his friend back.

Tom's head bounced from the corner of one of the servers and with a grunt he went limp and dropped to the floor. Instantly Mike was at his side, fingers searching for a pulse on the side of his dirty throat.

"Is he…" Leia's words trailed off, her eyes seeking Mikes, and he shook his head, relaxing slightly.

"He's just unconscious."

"What's wrong with him?"

"I don't know Leia, I really don't!" he admitted.

"We need to go," she stepped towards the door, watching as Mike and the young man joined her, a concerned look creeping onto her features as she studied the latter. "Are you going to be, OK?"

He nodded unconvincingly then the three of them were outside the server room and moving into the adjoining corridor only to freeze at what they saw.

Lining the glass walls of the offices that ran down the corridor on both sides, countless gamers were now stood against the windows, growling, and snarling at them, spittle and blood smearing the sheets of glass.

Their eyes turned to stare at the trio, frozen in shock and instantly fingernails began to scratch at the windows frantically, smearing the secretions there.

"It's like they've forgotten how to use doors," the young man muttered, head shaking in confusion.

"Mike, what's going on?" Leia fought to stay calm.

"I don't know," he shook his head, his eyes drifting to the distant elevator doors. "We need to get out of here before they remember how doors work."

With a nod from Mike the three of them began to move quickly down the corridor, their eyes locked to the elevator as they drew nearer to it, only to curse as the sounds of smashing glass and breaking furniture rang out. Hearts in their mouths they turned, fully expecting the windows to have been broken but they were all in one piece, keeping their occupants trapped.

Mike flinched as a blood curdling scream rose from the door to the right just ahead of them, followed by the sound of something wet hitting the floor, and casting them both a look of terror, Leia rushed toward the doorway and peered through into the room.

A woman lay curled in the foetal position against the far wall, covered in blood and sobbing like a child, while in the centre of the room two men were hunched over what appeared to be the bloody body of another woman. Pieces of glass littered the carpet around the trio, and as Leia stared in horror, she realised that the stomach of the woman had been torn open and that both the filth-caked men were sat gorging themselves on the thick sausage like entrails.

"Shit" Mike whispered as he joined Leia in the doorway, the young man hanging back, his back pressed firmly against the wall, perhaps in fear of another attack.

Mikes breathing was shallow, eyes wide as he stared at the horrific sight, before either of them had time to think of what to do the woman laying against the wall let out an animalistic growl and scrambled across the floor toward them both, blood now replacing the tears in her eyes.

Nine

"Run" Leia screamed to the young man behind them, as her and Mike backed away from the doorway and started running down the corridor toward the lift.

Sounds of shattering glass filled the corridor behind them as the gamers smashed their way out of their rooms, teeth bared. As Leia reached the threshold of the lift, she hit the call button, causing the doors to open with a mechanical groan, then hurried into the lift with Mike, stepping back as the young man smashed at the ground floor button while the snarling gamers ran toward the lift and the trio.

"The doors wont fucking shut in time," the young man cried out as he stumbled backward into the wall, falling hard onto the floor. "Fuck…FUCK!"

"Quick, give me a boost up to the maintenance hatch," Mike gestured to the ceiling above them, and exchanging glances, they did as he had instructed.

Grim faced, Mike managed to get the hatch to open and hauled himself up and through, then reached back down for Leias hands, grabbing her by the wrists. With a roar of determination, he leaned back, pulling her up just as the hoard of gamers rushed into the lift. The young man let out a scream of terror as they surrounded him, snarling and circling like a pack of wild animals ready to kill their pray.

Then Mike was leaning through the hatch once more, grasping at his arms and pulling him up while Leia hauled on the younger man's clothes. With a growl of denial, one of the gamers dived forwards, grabbing him by the exposed ankle as his jeans rode up, and sank his teeth deep within the fleshy tissue. The young man screamed in agony, and kicked hard with his free foot, feeling the crunch as it connected with the nose of the gamer who was now pulling away from his leg, a large chunk of pink tender flesh between its teeth, causing them to stumble backwards into the other snarling and reaching gamers, allowing the young lad to be pulled up into the shaft alongside Mike and Leia.

The lift started to tremble as the doors finally slid shut trapping the hoard in before making its slow descent down to the ground floor,

"The cunt bit me" the young man sobbed, grabbing at the wound on his ankle, "He bit me…he fucking bit me!"

"What's your name?" Leia asked him as the lift shuddered, about to reach the bottom of the shaft.

"Alex," he hissed in pain as he tried to rip a piece of fabric from his now torn trouser leg to try and cover the gaping wound, his features pale.

"I'm Leia and this is Mike, we're going to get you some help as soon as we can get out of here," she told him, in as calm a voice as she could manage, then he gasped as with a sudden lurch the lift stopped.

"Oh no!" Mike suddenly muttered from where he had been staring through the hatch down into the lift below, his features twisted in fear and confusion as he studied the snarling feral wretches that the gamers had become. "The people on this level!"

With a soft chime, the doors slid wide open and the three watched on in horror as the hoard of rage infested gamers rushed out of the lift into the building's lobby. A chorus of terrified screams and animalistic snarls and growls echoing back to them.

Ten

As they stood atop the elevator, Alex hissed as if he had felt a sudden sharp pain in the back of his head and sagged against the wall, grabbing at his temples. Sobbing in pain, he struggled to pull himself upright, blinking rapidly as if his vision had become blurred and he staggered forward to stare down through the hatch, fear in his voice. "They'll kill us. We got to get out of here now before they come back!"

Mike studied him for a moment, forcing a grim smile as the younger man met his gaze, then took a step back toward Leia, gently grabbing her by the arm and pulling her further away from Alex. Confused, she met his gaze, and he nodded toward the young man's face, his eyes now starting to leak blood. Stomach lurching in dread, Leia glanced back at Mike, her head starting to shake in denial, but he nodded, both their gazes dropping to study the bite wound in Alex leg.

The younger man suddenly seemed to feel the blood running from his eyes and raised his hands towards them, his fingertips coming away red, but then his pain intensified, and he suddenly crumpled forward as a violent fit racked through his lean body. Sobbing in agony he tried to stand, his hands reaching towards Mike and Leia as if pleading for help, then with a groan he fell sideways through the opening of the hatch, landing on the floor below unconscious.

"The bite did that…somehow this shit is infectious," Mike cursed under his breath, holding his head as he leaned back against the steel wall of the elevator shaft, his mind struggling to comprehend what had happened. For a few seconds, the world seemed to become silent, but then agonizing screams, breaking glass, and smashing furniture, snapped him back to reality. Forcing himself to focus, he realised that Leia was crouched beside the hatch, and he saw tears in her eyes as she met his gaze. "We need to help him!"

"He's turning in to one of those things," Mike stated, his right hand reaching out and gently trying to pull Leia away from the gap. "We can't help him now. Our only hope is to get down from here and past him before he wakes up and bites us too!"

"You're wrong!" Leia shook her head. "That doesn't make sense. They are all going crazy because of FRAY, it's not a vir..."

She gasped in shock, her words stopping short as a now infected Alex suddenly surged up from the floor, snarling and growling with the same feral rage that the others had displayed, teeth snapping.

He jerked his head up towards them as Leia gasped in dread, staring up through the lift hatch as they stood staring back down at him. Then with a feral snarl, the young man suddenly turned and raced out through the elevator door and into the lobby beyond.

"We need to get out of here!" Mike cursed.

"How?" Leia hated how scared she sounded as she replied. "Those things…Alex…"

"When we get down, we need to move quick, we don't know how many of these people are still in the lobby or how many more people have been infected," Mike explained as he crouched down beside the edge of the hatch and peered down. "It looks clear, but there could be some outside."

"What if there is?"

"Just hope there's not," he winced.
Carefully, Mike began lowering himself down through the hatch, landing softly in a crouch, then edged towards the doorway, his head peering around it.

Apparently satisfied that the corridor leading to the lobby was clear, Mike moved back then beckoned for Leia to join him, reaching up to help her down from the hatch. "Are you ready?"

She nodded, her face pale, and he sent her what he hoped was a reassuring smile, then turned and led her out into the main lobby beyond the elevator.

The security guard who had been there to greet them when they had first arrived now lay a little further down the corridor, his face nothing more than a bloody pulp, the contents of his skull smeared across the floor, chunks of brain mashed into the tiles.

Heading forward, leading Leia by the hand, Mike turned slowly, searching for any sign of danger then cursed as he spotted Alex rounding the corner a little further down the corridor. The young man froze as he saw them, dropping slightly into a crouch, and then began stalking them like a predator, his body close to the wall, sniffing the air as he came closer.

"Back, slowly," Mike's voice was a coarse whisper, and beside him, Leia's heart was in her mouth as she clutched at Mike's arm, pulling him toward a door just off to the right of them.

With a snarl, Alex suddenly charged them, his speed and disjointed staggering run filling them with terror. With a roar like a tiger, he hurled himself at them, slamming hard into Leia and sending her flying across the corridor into a door frame. She grunted in shock and fear as her head bounced off the wood with a dull thud and pain radiated across her skull. Trying to block out the ache, desperately trying to stay conscious, she lifted herself up and glanced over to see Mike grappling with Alex, the younger man trying to bite at her ex-boyfriend as if he were a rabid beast.

With a curse, Mike found himself beneath the infected man and brought his fist up hard on Alex's cheek bone causing his head to snap back, drawing a snarl of pain from him. Snapping teeth brushed past Mike's knuckles as he pulled his hand back and the younger man lost his balance, tripping over and falling heavily on his side. Heart hammering, Mike rolled to the side and straddled Alex's chest then grabbed him by the sides of his head, lifting it and then smashing it back down upon the tiled floor over and over, the dull thunk giving way to a wet thunk. Alex started to twitch violently as Mike smashed his head harder and harder upon the floor, his snarls now little more than grunts of shock and pain, his eyes barely even open.

With a sickening crack the back of the infected man's head finally gave way, his face seeming to lose its shape, and cursing in dread, Mike rose quickly and staggered back as a tar like substance began to run from the ruins of the dead man's skull, pooling about his body like a small sea of oil.

Fighting the urge to vomit, Leia rushed over to Mike and pulled him back away from the body of Alex toward the entrance to the building. "Come on!"

Mike couldn't shake the guilty feeling that he and Leia were responsible for all of this. They had been trying to save people and yet he was certain that by shutting down the servers he and Leia had only managed to make everything a thousand times worse.

ELEVEN

In moments they were walking again and turning the corner, the pair stopped in their tracks beside the security desk, their eyes wide as they took in the sight before them. The floor of the lobby was littered with shards of glass and broken furniture, strewn among countless mutilated bodies, some of them lying motionless on the carpet, their chest and stomachs ripped wide open, their organs strewn around them like discarded pieces of meat while the others lay gasping for breath or screaming and writhing in agony.

"Fuck," Leia gasped as she fought back a wave of nausea, her eyes starting to sting with tears as she looked down to see the bloody pulp of a child's face staring at them from the floor, the unfortunate girl looking to be no older than three years of age, her lifeless eyes staring off into the distance, her neck now nothing more than a raw fleshy wound where it would have once been connected to her small body.

Fighting his own nausea, Mike tried to usher Leia forward, knowing that at any possible moment the wounded writhing on the floor could turn into one of the rampaging beasts just as Alex had minutes before, but Leia couldn't take her eyes off the head.

From behind the pair, back in the main lobby, there was a chime as the elevator doors opened once more, then the muffled sounds of voices sounded as the office workers within exited out into the lobby.

As if on cue, the survivors of the attack by the gamers from the first elevator all started screaming in a twisted symphony, grabbing at their heads in unison as blood exuded from their eyes, only for the screams to quickly be replaced with snarls and excited grunts.

Screams of shock and fear suddenly sounded back in the foyer as the office workers who had travelled down in the elevator no doubt discovered the bloody remains of the security guard and Alex.

Several of the now infected survivors that could stand rushed snarling towards Leia and Mike, while the others raced off around the corner in the direction of the lobby and the office workers, screams of terror sounding as the groups came into sight of each other.

Cursing in dread, Mike shoved Leia to the side as a dwarf with pink hair rushed at the pair, her features disfigured from the violent attack she endured at the hands of the gamers. Her left eye socket was a bloody ruin and the orb that was once held within, now swung wildly on muscle as she ran at them.

The short woman collided with Mike, her teeth gnashing furiously as she tried to sink them in to his crotch, cursing in fear and shock, he raised a fist and punched her hard on the front of the forehead,

Filled with concern for Mike, Leia snatched up a ring of keys that were lying upon the security desk beside her and positioned them between her fingers then threw herself toward the pink haired woman. Eyes wide with fear, Mike shoved the little woman away from him, holding her at arms-length as Leia stepped in beside her and thrust her fist out, the keys stabbing into the attacker's throat. The keys punched through into the flesh, tearing deep into the pink-haired woman's windpipe. With a curse, Leia dragged her hand back, grimacing as the keys slipped free and the woman dropped to her knees gasping for breath, arterial blood spewing high from the wound.

As Mike and Leia staggered away from the dying pink haired woman, the fight between the office workers and the infected horde rounded the corner and they watched in shock as the entire corridor seemed to become blocked with men and women pushing and fighting with each other, the screams of the victims and the snarls of their attackers deafening.

As if reading each other's minds, they each ducked down behind the security desk, eyes wide as they studied the countless fights all around them.

TWELVE

"What the fuck Ken, stop being a prick and let me past!" a blonde middle-aged woman screeched as she tried to force her way through the middle of the melee, addressing the infected young Starbucks worker who she flirted with every morning only to back away as the horde seemed to surge towards her.

She cried out, staggering back into an older man who fell heavily to the floor, crying out in fear.

With a howl of terror, some of the surviving office workers tried to flee, and with a roar Starbuck's Ken jumped on top of the older man upon the floor, digging his fingers deep in to the eye sockets as the man screamed and writhed in agony, trying to fight him off, his legs kicking, his arms flailing uselessly.

With an almost suction like pop, the infected man scooped out an eyeball, held it up with an almost child-like grin, his teeth stained red with blood and then put it to his lips and sucked it in, savouring the taste as he bit into the gelatinous ball, blood-tinged vitreous jelly oozing from the sides of his mouth.

Maddened with pain, the writhing man managed to lift a knee, yet it collided weakly with Kens groin, drawing nothing more than a grunt from him as he started digging at the opposite eye socket.

With a scream, the middle-aged blonde woman tried to run as the horde charged after those trying to flee, yet her black fitting skirt was too tight to run in causing her to instead hobble across the corridor, only to be stopped as three of the infected surrounded her.

She cried out as an athletic black woman grabbed her violently by the shoulders from behind, dragging her down to the floor as two men dropped beside her, a giggling ginger man pinning her legs down while an overweight bearded man took great pleasure in ripping at her clothes. The blonde woman screamed hysterically as the one that had dragged her to the floor sank their teeth in to the side of her head and started shaking their face from side to side viciously, like a terrier killing a rat. The agony of the bite turned to a burning sensation across the side of her face as infected woman pulled back with her teeth, ripping off her ear and the skin around it.

The bearded man tearing at her clothes ripped her blouse open and pulled her bra down, exposing her body as the hot blood from her wound splashed down over her chest. Grabbing a hand full of her exposed right breast, he licked his lips then wrapped his bearded mouth around the globe of flesh within his hand, sucking in her nipple before closing his teeth and biting hard.

The woman let out a screech of pain and the ginger man holding her by the legs let out a hyena like chuckle, sliding a hand up her skirt, ripping his nails deep into her thigh, gouging five bloody furrows in her flesh. With a roar, he clenched his blood-soaked fingers and pushed them up between her legs, the woman's back arching in agony as he delved deep inside her body. She grunted, mouth opening and closing like a fish on dry land, so in pain that she was unable to scream, seemingly oblivious to the overweight man still biting into her breast and the woman eating her ear. Then with a triumphant grunt, the ginger man withdrew his fingers from her, a small fleshy misshapen object clasped in its bloody fingers.

THIRTEEN

In a matter of minutes, the office workers who had exited the lift lay scattered across the floor, some bleeding profusely, some unmoving, their bodies torn apart limb by limb.

Still crouched beside Leia, Mike turned his gaze over toward where the middle-aged woman was laying amid her trio of attackers, watching in horror as two of the infected gorged themselves on her flesh while the third grinned in excitement as it removed its hand from between the woman's legs, a fleshy shape clasped between its fingers.

For a moment the ginger infected man examined the meaty delicacy as it licked the blood trickling down their fingers from it then Mike suddenly felt a wave of nausea wash over him as he realised that the mass, the man had hold of was still somehow attached to the woman by a long tube-like structure that vanished back under her skirt. Eyes wide, he watched in horror as they raised it to their lips and took a bite from it, teeth ripping it in half before tossing it aside.

As Mike watched in horror, Leia raised herself beside the security desk, peering at the monitors that the security guard had been watching just a few hours beforehand to see if it showed the underground carpark or other areas of the building. Seeing nothing but the grey monitor, Leia grabbed the remote control from the desk and clicked the screen back on, clicking through the different camera streams until she found the underground carpark. As the image zoomed in Leia thought she saw movement coming out from under the barriers of the car park entrance, and cursing, she fumbled at the remote and hit the zoom button, paying close attention as the image focused on a figure moving swiftly through the gaps under the barriers, closely followed by a handful more. "Oh God, they are everywhere!"

"Shit" Mike uttered, as the infected further down the corridor stopped feasting and snarled at the sound of Leia's voice, turning in their direction.

"Run," Mike shouted as two of the infected surged to their feet and raced at him, knocking him off his feet and sending him crashing back, away from the lift area of the lobby, his body sliding on the tiled floor, stopping only as he collided with the wall.

Leia realised she no longer had hold of the keys and snatched them back up from where she had placed them moments before while hiding, grasping them tight in her hand, tucking a key between each finger, readying herself for an attack. She cursed as she saw Mike go crashing backwards and slide across the floor only to stop near the door to the car park, then cried out as she saw the two infected who had struck him now rushing toward her.

FOURTEEN

Heart in her mouth, Leia rushed around the security desk and ran toward the car park door, the pair of snarling infected close on her heels.

Forcing himself to his feet, Mike threw the door open as Leia approached. "Get in quickly!"

As they both exited the lobby into the stairwell, Mike slammed the door shut behind them, just as the two infected rushed toward it, closely followed by the rest of the horde, their snarling and grunting loud.

"We need to get out of here" Mike gasped, trying to steady himself as the adrenaline started to wear off. "We have to get to the car and make it as far away from here as possible."

Leia tensed, head shaking. "Mike there might be more infected people in the garage. I saw them on the monitor coming under the barrier from outside! We have to be careful down there!"

A loud crash suddenly sounded from the door beside them followed instantly by the sound of wood starting to creak and groan, and throwing each other concerned glances, Leia and Mike dashed down the stairs, hoping the door would hold for a while longer.

Another loud crash echoed down the stairwell to them as they hurried, followed by the sounds of splintering wood and then another deafening bang, then one last loud crash, followed by snarls and the sound of feet descending the stairs sounded above them.

Mike glanced back at Leia and smiled grimly as they reached the car park, relief showing clearly on his face as he saw his car a few rows from where they stood, parked beside a pillar. "We're almost there!"

Without warning, the horde made it to the bottom of the stairwell and spewed out into the car park, their snarls, and shrieks loud as they hunted.

"Shit, quick hide behind here," Leia cursed pointing to the large concrete pillar just ahead. "We have to get to the car without being seen."

The pair scurried behind a nearby car and getting on all fours they crawled across the concrete floor of the car park towards the large stone pillar.

They froze as a loud angry growl sounded off to the side, and turning they watched in dread as one of the infected moved into sight through the car window, sniffing at the air as if following their scent.

They turned their faces to the side as it moved out of sight, but its footsteps were clumsy and loud, and they could hear it slowly approaching them.

An animalistic howl rang out from somewhere off to their left, followed by a voice screaming something and footsteps echoing through the car park.

Screams echoed all around them and Leia raised her face to stare over the car bonnet towards the noise, realising as she did so that the figures she had seen sneaking under the barrier on the security camera must have been people and not more infected.

"Mike, we need to help them!" she lurched to her feet beside the car, catching the attention of the infected individual who had been just a few feet away.

It snarled and threw itself across the car bonnet it was stood beside and made a grab for Leia, its fingers just brushing her shoulder as she jumped to the side and cursing Mike was about to get to his feet when he noticed something under a car just to the right of him. Grimacing, he stretched his arm toward it and scraped at the object until he managed to get it free from where it had been partially under a tyre.

Heart racing, he tightened his grip around the broken windscreen wiper arm that he was now brandishing as a weapon and lunged toward the infected man who had given up trying to catch Leia and was now on the floor scrambling toward him.

With a snarl of his own, Mike thrust out with the wiper, the metal arm of it lancing deep within the infected man's right eye causing it to let out a shriek. Fighting the urge to vomit, Mike twisted the wiper before pulling it back toward him, leaving a ragged wound, blood cascading down the infected man's face, then raising the wiper blade again Mike drove it deep into the man's throat, severing the artery. Blood pumped out as the infected staggered to its feet and crashed back, falling against the pillar.

Mike cried out in shock as hands grabbed at him, blinking as he found Leia trying to drag him to his feet. "Come on Mike!"

Screams echoed throughout the car park as Leia and Mike slowly made their way along the line of cars, heading toward the area the screams had come from, then Leia grabbed Mikes arm, gesturing for him to stop as she held a finger to her lips then pointed toward the back of a car just ahead of them where two dark figures were crouching, huddled together.

"I don't know if you are one of them but get away from my me and my sister," a voice warned them, and exchanging glances, they edged closer.

"We're not infected and neither of us have been bitten," Mike called out. "I promise you that."

"We can help you" Leia added walking toward them, extending her free hand outwards.

The smaller of the two stood up, followed by the other and then the pair stepped away from the car they were hiding behind, the taller of the two stumbling toward Mike and Leia. "Please help us!"

"Shit, they are kids," Leia grunted in shock, then forced herself to focus. "What are your names?"

The taller of the two winced as if unsure whether to tell her then turned to study his younger sibling, as she stood looking at the ground, her shoulders sagging, then he met Leia's questioning gaze once more. "I am Luke, this is Ava."

"Where are your parents?" Mike asked them.

Luke shrugged. "At work, we are on a school trip, we got chased in here by some crazy people outside who tried to attack our group, our teacher thought this was the best place to hide out but then there were more crazy people in here too."

Leia suddenly stiffened as she caught sight of movement off in the corner of her eye, tightening her grip on the keys that she still clutched in her fist, shifting her weight slightly so she could ready herself for whatever came next. Turning her head, squinting in the direction the movement had come from, she saw three shadows moving closer "Oh fuck no!"

Ushering Leia and the two children back into the shelter of the car's shadows, Mike tensed waiting for the attack. The three figures stepped closer, snarling, and baring their teeth, and Ava let out a squeal of terror as Luke pulled her closer to him.

"Get ready to run," Mike told Leia and the pair, as he stepped between them and the snarling trio.

FIFTEEN

The infected rushed forward, the first barging Leia to the ground, knocking the breath from her as she landed hard. The second darted toward Mike as he shouted to the youngsters to run, and with a snarl, the third gave chase after the two screaming children.

Leia raised her right hand, her keys still tightly gripped between her fingers, and jabbed repeatedly at the face and neck of the infected that was crouching over her, the keys sinking deep within their cheek.

With a roar of pain, it reared off balance and fell backwards. Heart in her mouth, Leia rolled to her knees and mounted their chest, stabbing down hard in their throat, over and over, blood covering her face. The infected gasped for breath as a blow severed their windpipe, the skin around it sucking tight as they struggled to breathe, the rasping sound awful to hear.

Rising and stepping back, Leia turned to find Mike wrestling with the infected that had charged him.

Gritting her teeth, she rushed over and grabbed it by the hair, holding its head back just as it was about to bite Mike, allowing him to kick out and knock the legs from beneath it. Grasping at Mikes hand the pair stepped back, knowing that they needed to get away and find the children but also realising that this infected was going to give chase if they didn't stop it.

Cursing loudly, Mike stepped forwards and kicked the infected hard in the chest as it tried to rise, causing it to fall back to the ground while Leia kicked it in the head, over and over. It snarled, turning to grasp at her shoe and Mike raised his foot above it, his heavy black boot slamming down upon the rib cage.

There was a sickening crunch as the ribs cracked beneath his foot, and raising his foot he stomped again this time harder, his boot sinking deeper into the chest cavity than it had before as the sternum gave way. Stepping back, Leia watched in dread as Mike stamped hard down again, and the infected stopped moving, blood oozing from the sides of its mouth. Yet Mike couldn't stop himself, he had to keep stomping, harder and harder until the flesh split and his foot slipped inside. Leia let out a gasp followed by the urge to vomit as she realised it now looked as if Mike was wearing the infected carcass as some form of footwear as he stood ankle deep in it.

Mike threw her a weak smile before removing his leg, the skin sloughing up around his boot as he did so, unidentifiable pieces of organs stuck within the tread of his bloody shoe. "We need to find the kids." Side-by-side, they edged deeper into the car park as screams began to echo all around them. Peeking around a corner while Mike watched their rear, Leia frowned as she studied a group of small figures huddled around something upon the ground.

"Please help us!" one of the figures cried out as it spotted her. "There are lots of them and we don't know what to do. They attacked us and one of them bit our teacher!"

"More kids!" Mike realised, and exchanging glances, he and Leia stepped out from the corner just as two infected rushed into view, rushing toward the group of children, while in their centre a figure on the ground began screaming and convulsing violently.

"We need to help them!" Mike exclaimed as he rushed past Leia, his fear forgotten in concern for the youngsters. The figure on the ground among them suddenly snarled and rose on all fours, then pounced forward, knocking one of the children off their feet.

As Leia watched in horror, the infected teacher bent forward mouth agape, closing it over the centre of the child's face, teeth sinking deep. Screams muffled by the attack, the child clawed at the infected teacher's arms as the woman pulled her head backward slowly, the tender flesh of the youngster's face stretching, before the flesh ripped free, peeling away to reveal a red pulpy mass of muscle underneath.

The other children stood screaming in terror, frozen to the spot as the two male infected rushed at them, and in desperation Mike yelled at the kids to run but it was far too late.

Snarling, the pair of infected men crashed into the group of terrified children, like a pair of lions amid a herd of zebra, and as the teacher continued to feast upon the now faceless body of the girl, the men went crazy, biting and scratching the screaming youngsters.

Filled with a terrible fury, Mike grabbed one of the men by the shoulders, dragging it back as Leia appeared beside him, her hands trembling as the anguished cries of the children pierced the air. Leia felt a rush of rage wash over her as she lunged at the other infected man who was clawing at a small ginger girl, her pale freckled face and throat covered in deep bloody furrows as the man tore at her face and body.

As the snarling man spun to face her, Leia punched him hard in the side of the head only for the man to grunt weakly as if it had done no harm at all, and in desperation she swung her right leg at it. The blow struck it below the left knee, knocking the limb sideways at an angle that nature had never intended, and the infected man fell to the ground, its body twisting as it reached for her, lips drawn back as it snarled in hatred and anger. A raised kerb caught the infected man as he landed, a sickening crack sounding as his forehead struck the edge of the stone block.

Head shaking in disbelief, Leia staggered back, eyes wide as she stared at the dead man, then turned to the young girl that he had been attacking, her heart twisting in grief as she saw that the child had bled out.

Stepping back, she turned to see that Mike was still struggling with the man he had pulled off one of the young children, the pair wrestling violently.

As Leia watched, the man twisted around to face Mike, grabbing him by the arms and forcing him backwards to crash into the side of a parked car. Desperately trying not to fall, Mike whipped both arms up and outward in a circular motion breaking the infected man's grip on him, knocking him back several steps, before bending at the waist and charging him.

His shoulder made contact with the infected man's stomach, knocking him back to the floor, and as he landed, the small child who Mike had just saved rushed over and started kicking hard at the infected.

Mike watched as the young boy pulled something from his pocket, his fingers fumbling to open it, and as a glint of metal caught Mike's eye, the child dropped to his knees beside the infected man.

Then with a snarl, the boy began to stab at the infected repeatedly with what Mike now realised was a Swiss army knife, blood coating the child's hand.

Snarling, the infected slapped the young boy across the face, knocking him off his feet and Mike stepped forward and kicked the man hard in the head, before raising his foot and bringing it down with great force upon his face, over and over until he felt the man's skull give way beneath his boot, killing the infected.

He tensed as Leia grasped at him, drawing him back, both their gaze's falling upon the infected teacher who had carried on eating the now faceless child that she had attacked. Silently, the pair moved forwards, grabbing at the two remaining children, a boy and a girl and led them to the safety of Mike's car.

Loading the children into the vehicle, telling them to keep quiet, the pair made their way through the rows of cars, desperately trying to find Luke and Ava, knowing if they called out to them, they would alert any other infected that may still be in the vicinity.

For what seemed an eternity, they continued walking and checking cars, and then, just when Leia was about to suggest giving up they found the pair, tucked away in a doorway. Grim-faced, Mike and Leia stood side-by-side, studying the young pair as they sat there, Luke with his sister's head on his lap, stroking her hair, and telling her everything would be okay.

On shaky legs, Leia moved to stand beside the pair, trying to hold back the tears as she looked into the lifeless eyes of Ava, her eyes wide and bloodshot.

Luke glanced up at her, then kissed his little sister gently upon the forehead. "Ava wake up, we are safe now. We can go home and see mum and dad"

"Luke," Leia started, her voice breaking.

"Ava, come on, wake up," he repeated, shaking her gently. "Wake up please, I told you they would find us, wake up! Please, come on…Ava…AVA!"

Mike walked over to the young girl and gently picked her lifeless body up from her brother's arms, tears stinging at his cheeks as he met Luke's gaze. "I am so sorry."

"We ran just like you told us too," Luke spoke as if answering some unspoken question. "We hid here but Ava was crying loudly and two of them angry people came round, I covered her mouth to keep them from finding us and she fell asleep but now she won't wake up!"

SIXTEEN

A sudden roar echoed through the car park, and something crashed loudly over to the left of them, causing Luke to flinch and rush to Leias side.

Mike was about to explain to the boy what had happened to his sister when he noticed Leia's facial expression change to one of panic then he felt someone grabbing him from behind.

With a curse of fear, he staggered backwards, dropping Ava's limp body as whoever it was pulled at him. Fearing the sensation of teeth tearing into his neck from behind, Mike tried to struggle free, but the grasp was too strong, and he felt himself being pulled to the ground. With a roar of denial, Leia threw herself at the infected which was grappling with Mike, her head colliding with the woman's head, the impact knocking her face down toward Mikes chest.

Desperately trying to pull her away from him, Leia yanked at the woman's hair dragging her head back away from his chest, giving Mike enough room to bring his head forward and strike the woman hard on the bridge of the nose, rocking her backwards.

Mind reeling, Luke stood watching in horror as the trio grappled around his sister's lifeless body, his confusion and fear combining to fuel him with anger.

"Get away from my sister!" he screamed loudly, running over, and kicking out at the infected woman, snatching her attention just long enough for Leia to wrap her hands around the woman's waist and throw her to the ground. Leia jumped on top of the snarling woman as she tried to get to her feet, then grabbing her by the back of the head she smashed her face into the concrete ground, over and over each hit sounding wetter than the last, lifting her head and smashing it harder against the concrete each time and leaving the woman's face nothing more than a pulpy mess, teeth littering the ground. With a groan, Leia rolled off the woman and got to her feet, stumbling over to where Mike still lay on the ground. "Are you OK?"

He grunted, smiling wearily as he met her gaze, and she gave a groan of relief as she took one of his hands and helped him stand. "Thank God. I thought she got you!"

Mike shook his head then turned to stare sadly at Luke who was now sat beside his sister's lifeless body, sobbing. "She's not going to wake up is she? I hurt her didn't I?"

Throat tight with emotion, Leia lifted him into an embrace. "We need to go. I am so sorry."

"What?" he was horrified. "We can't leave her!"

"We have to," she told him softly, her voice breaking once more as she spoke. "I am so sorry."

Then on legs that felt like lead, Leia and Mike, and the sobbing Luke, made their way back toward Mike's car where the other two children were still hiding.

The walk back to the car felt like a lifetime, Mike hanging back slightly behind Leia and the boy as they reached the car, struggling with his emotions.

Leia let out a sigh of relief to see the two other children were still safe within the vehicle, their faces lighting up with sad smiles as they saw their classmate.

Moments later, and all three kids were sat safely in the car as Leia looked back at Mike, a sad smile upon her face. "We need to get out of here."

SEVENTEEN

The group sat in silence as they made their way out of the car park, Mike, and Leia now both feeling the effects of the day and its events in the front of the vehicle, and the three classmates in the rear.

Leia's eyes flickered to Mike's face several times as he steered the car through the gloomy car park, the weariness evident on his face and she was sure that her own face had begun to show the same signs.

Glancing at the clock on the dashboard, Leia was stunned to see it was only five pm. It felt like they had been fighting to escape the building for days.

As they drove out of the car park, and began to drive through the city, Leia watched in dread as they passed people running in every direction, many being chased by infected people, while there were countless cars abandoned in the roads, and bodies lay scattered everywhere they looked, half eaten or wounded.

Turning to tell the three children in the back to close her their eyes, Leia let out a gasp as she noticed that the boy who she and Mike had saved from their teacher had what appeared to be a bite on his arm.

"Mike, I think one of them has a bite," she whispered, hoping the children wouldn't hear her.

"Miss is there something wrong?" the little boy asked sounding alarmed as he fidgeted with the sleeve on his top trying to cover the wound on his arm.

Turning in her seat, Leia tried to remain calm as she forced a smile. "Did one of the people bite you?"

"A man did," he admitted, sounding ashamed.

"Then he bit Miss Wheatley," Luke added.

Mike glanced at Leia. "If he got bit before the teacher, he should have become one of those fucking things by now unless…nah surely not."

"What? Leia asked

"The kid could be immune to whatever the virus is," he replied, a strange smile on his features.

"What?"

"The kid could be immune to whatever the virus is," he replied, searching his mind for the information he wanted to back up his theory.

Leias expression shifted from confused to sceptical. "But why would that happen?"

Mike shrugged. "Well kids under the age of twelve aren't meant to play VR games due to the idea it will affect their brain function, maybe the virus that has changed everyone only affects older brains."

The confused expression remained on Leia's face. "I don't follow what you're trying to say."

Mike sighed. "I think he might be immune."

"Either way, we need to get these kids back to their parents or the police," Leia stated then glanced round to find the child who had been bitten now sat trembling, his forehead covered in beads of sweat and his complexion almost grey. "Are you okay?"

"Miss, I think I'm going to be sic..." he started, only to be interrupted by the contents of his stomach exiting his body at high velocity, spraying the two children sat beside him in hot acrid fluid. Staring wide eyed at Leia, the little girl burst into tears as the young boy sat between her and Luke, threw up again, the smell causing Luke to gag. The young boy slumped forward, his breathing becoming ragged as he began to convulse as if having a seizure.

Leia and Mike had no time to react before the boy suddenly snarled and turned on the young girl sat beside him, his teeth tearing into her throat. She tried to scream, the sound a gargled choke as she tried to push him away, only for his fingers to find her eyes, pushing deep as he worked his teeth on her throat.

Blood sprayed up the interior of the car, and sobbing in terror, Luke unclipped his seat belt and tried to scramble into the front seat to get away.

Mike slammed the brakes on in shock, and Luke flew forward, smashing his head into the back of Leia's, causing her to jerk forwards and hit her face off the windshield, knocking her unconscious. Then suddenly another car was there, skidding wildly before it slammed hard into the back of Mikes car.

The sudden impact, threw Mike sideways, smashing the side of his head off the driver's window, shattering the glass, his vision fading as he too slipped into unconsciousness.

EIGHTEEN

Leia awoke to a horn blaring, and for a moment she sat in a daze, trying to remember what had happened only to curse as she recalled the infected boy.

Groaning, she turned in her chair to find that the infected boy was dead, a long shard of broken glass through his throat, while the unfortunate young girl had died from the deep bite wounds to her throat.

She glanced sideways as Mike started to stir, then turned back once more as she heard sobs coming from the back footwell, unbuckling her seat belt as she stared down at a pale-faced Luke. "Are you OK?"

"I hurt my head," he sobbed, tears rolling down his face. "I want my mum and dad. I want Ava!"

With a groan, Mike climbed out of the car and stumbled around to the passenger side, throwing open the back door he helped the child out then turned to study the vehicle that had driven into them.

The driver of the car that had hit them nowhere in sight but there was blood on the road.

He glanced back as Leia climbed out of the car and moved alongside him and Luke. "What now"

"Honestly? I don't know," Mike just wanted the nightmare to be just that, to wake up at home in bed and find it was all a bad dream. But then he felt Luke trembling against his side and realized he was wrong; this nightmare wasn't going to end any time soon.

About the Author

Renn White is a horror fanatic and writer from Northumberland. She spends most of her free time roaming the woods, collecting inspiration for her horror stories. Renn's love of taxidermy and all things macabre shines through in her writing. As a self-described "horror fanatic," Renn draws from a wide range of influences, from classic horror literature to B-rated horror movies. Her writing aims to elicit both fear and wonder in her readers, tapping into the darkness that lurks within all of us.

Printed in Great Britain
by Amazon

33750484R00054